TINY TOWNS AND OTHER PLACES WE CALL HOME

Story by **Mary Ann Wilson**

Illustrations by **Abigail Wilson**

To order additional copies of this book, contact:
Xlibris
1-888-795-4274
www.Xlibris.com
Orders@Xlibris.com

ISBN:	Softcover	978-1-7960-8448-1
	Hardcover	978-1-7960-8449-8
	EBook	978-1-7960-8447-4

Library of Congress Control Number: 2020901437

Print information available on the last page

Rev. date: 02/04/2020

Some people live in tiny towns.

A tiny town means different things to different people.

A town like this could feel small to some, and HUGE to other people.

Very few people live in tiny towns.

Houses can be very far apart.

To me, the coolest thing about living in a place like this would be……

ALL THOSE STARS!

In some tiny towns, it would probably be harder to visit your friends, but when you did, there would be so many exciting things to do…

like explore trails… and ride bikes…and pretend that your bikes were horses like the ones people rode in the Wild West!

Maybe you could even catch some fish,

or a WHOLE LOT of FISH!

It could also get a little lonely and you might wish you lived in a different kind of town…

One where your best friends lived next door, and by that, I mean, NEXT DOOR.

The first thing you'll notice is the noise.

It's not bad or scary, it's just noise…that after a while, you'll barely hear anymore. You might even feel a little lost when you can't hear that comforting buzz of traffic, people talking, and music of all kinds.

Did you know that even streetlights make noise?

CALL NOW!

There would be lots and lots of kids in your school. Even if your town was so small that you could ride your bike from one end of town to the other, there would still be lots of kids.

After all, this kind of town doesn't take up much space.

YOURTOWN ELEMENTARY SCHOOL

And summers… Aw yeah!!!

I could smell the hot dogs, burgers and chicken right now.

Mmmmm…

Anyway, I used to spend lots of time wanting to be somewhere else… Anywhere else.

Laying in my bed, imagining that I was under stars instead of streetlights.

Then, like a soft, warm blanket that covered me from head to toe, I realized that I could be…That I WAS anywhere I wanted to be, in my head, in my thoughts, in my heart.

The place you find in your imagination can be real too.

What's in your heart is what makes you happy… RIGHT WHERE YOU ARE.

OUR SOLAR SYSTEM

CPSIA information can be obtained
at www.ICGtesting.com
Printed in the USA
BVHW020939140220
572397BV00010B/254